Thank You, God

Written by **Charlotte Lundy**

Illustrated by **Miriam Sagasti**

"This book is dedicated to our son, Brad, and his love of flying."

THANK YOU, GOD

Text Copyright © 2005 by Charlotte Lundy
Illustrations Copyright © 2005 by Miriam Sagasti

The illustrations in this book were rendered in watercolor.

FIRST PRINTING

Published by Bay Light Publishing, Inc.
        Mooresville, North Carolina

Layout and Production by Heather Claremont Sullivan
        6925 Brandon Chase Lane, Concord, NC 28025

Printed in Korea

Publisher's Cataloging-in-Publication
(Provided by Quality Books, Inc.)

Lundy, Charlotte.
      Thank You, God / Charlotte Lundy, author;
Miriam Sagasti, illustrator; Evelyn L. Waldrep, editor. --1 st ed.
      p. cm.
      Includes bibliographical references.
      SUMMARY: Patrick dreams of flying airplanes. When a
flight instructor tells him he's a natural at flying, Patrick's father
tells him about how God gives us all natural talents in life.
      Audience: Ages 4-8.
      ISBN 0-9670280-9-4

      1. Airplanes--Juvenile fiction. 2. Ability in
children--Juvenile fiction. 3. God--Juvenile fiction.
[1. Airplanes--Fiction. 2. Ability--Fiction. 3. God--
Fiction. 4. Individuality--Fiction.]
I. Sagasti, Miriam. II. Waldrep, Evelyn L. III. Title.

PZ7.L97887Tg 2004   [E]
                                  QBI33-542

Former US President Jimmy Carter
proudly holds the 2002 Nobel Peace Prize
he received in Oslo, Norway.

"A Child's Prayer"

Dear God,

Thank you for giving each of us
special talents.

Please lead and guide me
throughout my life
to use my special talents
to honor you.

Amen

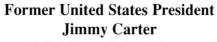

Former United States President
Jimmy Carter
Nobel Peace Prize Winner
Humanitarian-Mediator
Plains, Georgia

It all started when I was six years old...my love for airplanes!

My name is Patrick, and I can remember lying in the grass in our backyard watching airplanes fly over our house during the annual Air Show at the Air Force Base in our hometown.

My dream then was to become a pilot.

The closest thing to flying an airplane at my age was flying the paper airplanes I made from notebook paper at school. Some of those airplanes could really fly!

When I was about ten years old, my father realized
how much I liked airplanes. He asked me if I would like to build
and fly remote controlled airplanes. Of course, he knew what my
answer would be. YES! For several years, we built and flew many
different types of remote controlled airplanes. That was so much fun
and taught me a lot about flying.

When I turned twelve years old, my father said that he had a friend who owned an airplane out at the local airport and that he would take me for a ride if I would like to go. I couldn't believe my ears! WOW! A real airplane ride. Of course I wanted to go.

The next weekend my dad and I met his friend, Mr. Omohundro, at the local airport. He owned a Beechcraft Sundowner. His airplane was beautiful. We all got in the plane and took off. I couldn't believe my eyes. This was the first time that I had seen the earth from an airplane. We were so high and I could see everything.

All of the land down below us was so different than I had imagined!

The farms, houses and highways were all lined-up and squared-off. I could see for miles and miles! Everything that seemed so big on the ground looked so small from up where we were.

I had the time of my life riding in the airplane that day. It was then that I realized that one day I was going to be a pilot.

When I was about fourteen years old, I asked my father
if I could take flying lessons. He said that if I got a job and paid for
half of them that we could work out a deal for me to take flying lessons.

So that's what I did. I got a job at the local airport pumping gas,
washing airplanes, and running errands that paid just enough for half
of my flying lessons.

My dream was finally coming true. After passing the written exam and flying for several months, my instructor said that I was "a natural." I asked my dad what he meant by this.

He said, "When we are born, God gives us all special talents for us to use in our lives. Each and every one of us has a special talent."

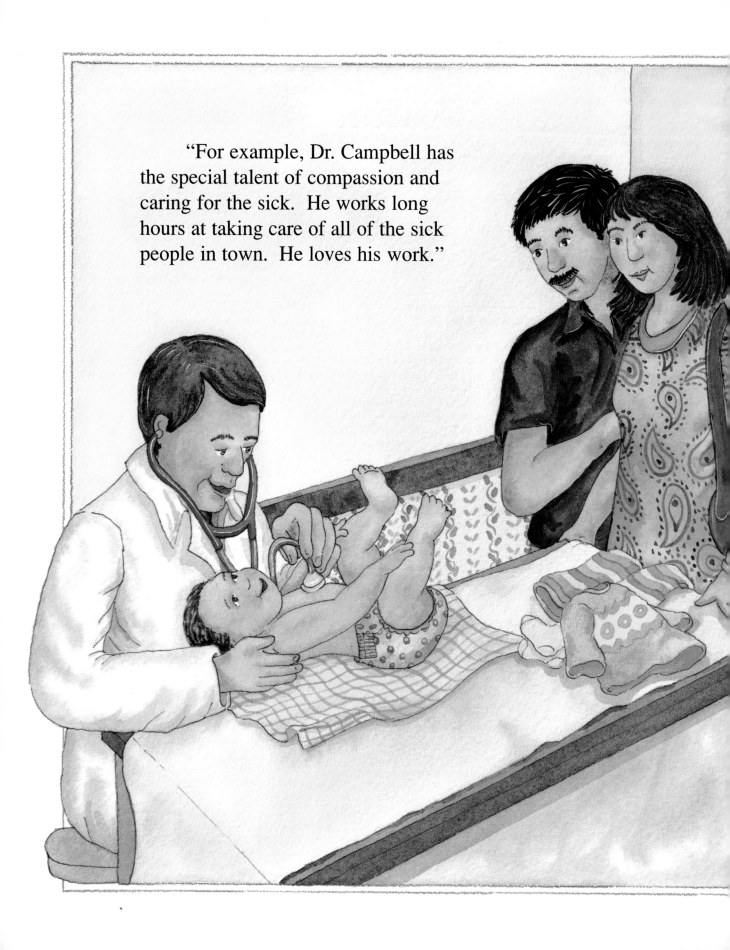

"For example, Dr. Campbell has the special talent of compassion and caring for the sick. He works long hours at taking care of all of the sick people in town. He loves his work."

"Our neighbor, Mrs. Hankins, has the special talent of feeding and caring for the hungry. She is always down at the Christian Soup Kitchen cooking and feeding the people who are hungry."

"God gave Mr. Wilson the special talent to build houses.
He works very hard for Habitat For Humanity to help build new homes
for the poor and needy."

"I believe that God gave me the talent to take care of this farm. I love mowing the fields, growing corn, and taking care of all the animals."

"I believe with all of my heart that God has given you the talent to fly airplanes. When Mr. Baker tells you that you are "a natural," he means that God has given you the natural ability to understand and fly airplanes."

When I was sixteen years old, I flew my solo flight all by myself in the airplane. It had been two years since I had started taking flying lessons.

I was so excited and proud that I had become a pilot. My dream had finally come true!

After I had landed and parked the airplane, I got out, looked up to the sky and said, "Thank You, God, for giving me the special talent to fly airplanes."

The End

"We salute the men and women who serve and protect our country at home and around the world."